MW00763437

Who Made That Sound?
Animals
and their sounds in English, Spanish, and Mandarin

Address inquiries to Contact@florenza.org

Paperback ISBN 978-1-941328-64-4
Hardcover ISBN 978-1-941328-55-2
eBook ISBN 978-1-941328-63-7

Library of Congress Number 2022934932

Words to Ponder Publishing Company, LLC

We dedicate this book to all the children in the world.

This Book Belongs to:

_____

Stay curious
Love, Amy

thank you♡

Alligators hiss and bellow.

Los caimanes sisean y gruñen.

鳄鱼嘶嘶和低吼。

Bears growl and roar.

Los osos gruñen y rugen.

熊怒吼和咆哮。

Bees buzz.

Las abejas zumban.

蜜蜂嗡嗡。

Buffalos mumble and grunt.

Los búfalos murmullan y gruñen.

水牛嘀咕和嘟哝。

Cats meow and purr.

Los gatos maúllan y ronronean.

猫喵喵和呼噜声。

Chickens cluck and cha-caw.

Los pollos pían y cloquean.

鸡咯咯哒。

Cows moo.

Las vacas mugen.

母牛哞哞。

Dogs bark and woof.

Los perros ladran y hacen guau guau.

狗吠和汪汪。

Dolphins click.

Los delfines chasquean.

海豚咔嗒声。

Donkeys hee-haw and bray.

Los burros hacen iii-aah y rebuznan.

驴嗯昂和嘶叫。

Ducks quack.

Los patos graznan.

鸭子嘎嘎。

Elephants trumpet.

Los elefantes barritan.

大象喇叭声。

Foxes howl and scream.

Los zorros aúllan y gritan.

狐狸尖声嚎叫。

Grizzly bears huff and growl.

Los osos Grizzly resoplan y gruñen.

灰熊吐气和怒吼。

Hippopotamuses growl.

Los hipopótamos gruñen.

河马怒吼。

Horses neigh and whinny.

Los caballos relinchan y resoplan.

马儿嘶鸣。

Hummingbirds hum and chirp.

Los colibríes zumban y gorjean.

蜂鸟嗡嗡和叽喳。

Koalas bellow and shriek.

Los koalas rugen y chillan.

考拉低吼和尖叫。

Mice squeak.

Los ratones chillan.

老鼠吱吱。

Monkeys scream.

Los monos gritan.

猴子尖叫。

Owls hoot.

Los búhos ululan.

猫头鹰咕咕喵。

Pandas squeak and huff.

Los pandas chillan y resoplan.

熊猫吱吱和吐气。

Pigs squeal and oink.

Los cerdos chillan y hacen oink oink.

猪叽叽和哼哼。

Rabbits squeak.

Los conejos chirrean.

兔子吱吱。

Raccoons trill.

Los mapaches ronronean.

浣熊发颤声。

Rhinoceroses moo and grunt.

Los rinocerontes mugen y gruñen.

犀牛呜呜和嘟哝。

Roosters cock-a-doodle-doo.

Los gallos hacen quiquiriquí.

公鸡喔喔。

Sheep baa and meh.

Las ovejas hacen beee.

羊儿咩咩。

Snakes hiss and rattle.

Las serpientes sisean y cascabelean.

蛇嘶嘶和响尾。

Swans trumpet and bugle.

Los cisnes trompetean y graznan.

天鹅喇叭和号角声。

Tigers roar and growl.

Los tigres rugen y gruñen.

老虎咆哮和怒吼。

Turkeys gobble.

Los pavos gluglutean.

火鸡咯咯。

Wolves howl and bay.

Los lobos aúllan y ladran.

狼嚎叫和长鸣。

Published titles by Florenza are:

Adventurous Olivia's Alphabet Quest
Adventurous Olivia's Calm Quest: A Book on Mindfulness
Adventurous Olivia's Numerical Quest
Amiri's Birthday Wish
Barry Bear's Very Best, Learning to Say No to Negative Influences
Brooklyn Beaver ALMOST Builds a Dam
If...The Story of Faith Walker
Manny & Tutu
Mind Your Manners, Mia
Purpose: Life According to God's Plan
There's No Place Like My Own Home
The Tail of Max the Mindless Dog, A Children's Book on Mindfulness
This Time Next Year: A Friendship Story
Welcome Home Daddy, Love, Lexi
When Life Gives Us Wind

Children's Books coming soon are:
Acornsville, Land of the Secret Seed Keepers
Adventurous Olivia's Numerical Quest
Micah and Malik's Super Awesome Excellent Adventure
Oh, My Goodness, Look at this Big Mess
Two Bees in a Hive

Young Reader Chapter Books coming soon are:
Hoku to the Rescue
Two-Thirds is a Whole

For more information regarding Florenza's books, or to contact her to speak at your school or event,

please visit www.florenza.org.

A pig by any other name is still a pig.

Un cerdo con cualquier otro nombre sigue siendo un cerdo.

不管把猪叫什么它还是猪。

Who Made That Sound: Animals and their sounds in English, Spanish, and Mandarin
introduces young readers to the fascinating world of language
through beautifully illustrated images of easily recognizable animals.
From a mooing cow to a gobbling turkey, your child will want to read this book again and again.

¿Quién hizo ese sonido? Animales y sus sonidos en inglés, español y mandarín
introduce a los jóvenes lectores al fascinante mundo del lenguaje a través de imágenes
bellamente ilustradas de animales fácilmente reconocibles.
Desde una vaca que muge hasta un pavo que gluglutea, su hijo querrá leer este libro una y otra vez.

谁发出了那个声音：动物和它们的声音 – 英文、西班牙文和中文，通过精美插图和极易识别的动物，把神奇的语言世界介绍给年轻的读者。从哞哞叫的母牛到咯咯喊的火鸡，你的孩子会一遍又一遍地读这本书。